Hansel and Gretel

Illustrated by Alida Massari

BONNEY PRESS

Published by Bonney Press,
an imprint of Hinkler Books Pty Ltd
45–55 Fairchild Street
Heatherton Victoria 3202 Australia
www.hinkler.com.au

BONNEY
PRESS

© Hinkler Books Pty Ltd 2016

Illustration: Alida Massari
Text: Katie Hewat
Design: Paul Scott and Pooja Desai
Editorial: Emily Murray

ISBN: 978 1 4889 0491 2

Printed and bound in China

Hansel
and
Gretel

Once upon a time there lived a poor woodcutter, his wife, and his two children named Hansel and Gretel.

Though the woodcutter loved his children very much, his **wicked wife** wished them gone. There was a great famine throughout the land and she did not want to share what little food they had with her two *lousy* stepchildren.

One night, as the woodcutter worried over how he would feed his family, his wife told him, 'Do not worry, husband, for I have found some work for the children and myself at a house on the other side of the forest. I will take the children tomorrow and we will bring home a fine dinner.'

But Hansel, who lay awake in his bed, overheard this. He remembered the time that his stepmother had tried to sell him to a peddler in exchange for a new hat, and the time that she had tricked him into believing a nearby beehive was empty. He knew **she was up to no good.**

So the next morning, before they set out, Hansel filled his pockets with small brown pebbles from the garden.

As his stepmother led them through the forest, Hansel sprinkled a pebble here and a pebble there, creating a trail he could easily follow back home.

After many miles, Hansel and Gretel's stepmother turned to them and said, 'You poor children look thirsty. Wait here and I will fetch some water for you,' and she disappeared into the woods.

After some time, Hansel realised that he and his sister were stranded. Gretel began to cry, as little sisters often do. **'Fear not,'** said Hansel. **'I know the way.'** And they followed the path of pebbles home.

Hansel and Gretel arrived to find their father beside himself with worry. 'Your stepmother told me how you became separated. I thought you were **lost forever!**' he cried, pulling them both into a *fierce* hug.

Their stepmother, though really quite furious, pretended to be relieved. 'We shall set out again tomorrow,' she sighed, 'but this time we will make sure **everything** goes to plan.'

The following morning, Hansel and Gretel's stepmother woke them *very* early. She handed them each a piece of bread as their breakfast, and led them into the forest.

Hansel, having had no time to collect pebbles, but certain of what his stepmother was planning, broke the bread into little pieces and left a *trail of breadcrumbs* on the ground as they walked.

This time, their stepmother led them into a *deeper* part of the forest. After a long time, Gretel's legs became tired from walking so they all decided to rest by the trunk of a big tree. The children soon fell asleep.

When they awoke, it was **dark** and their stepmother was gone. Hansel built a small fire to keep them warm and told Gretel he would lead them home in the morning.

When daylight came, they set off along the path they had travelled the day before, but the breadcrumbs had disappeared. Hansel soon realised that the forest animals must have eaten them. 'Well, *that* was a **stupid idea**', he thought. They were totally and utterly lost. Gretel began to cry.

At that moment, they heard a *sweet song* coming from a nearby tree. Looking around in surprise, Gretel saw a snow white bird sitting on a low branch and swallowed her tears to watch it. When the bird flitted out of the tree and into the forest, Gretel ran after it, and Hansel followed close behind. The beautiful bird led them to a clearing in the forest.

Standing in the middle of the clearing was a beautiful cottage made from gingerbread, and *covered in sweets*. It was the most exquisite thing Hansel and Gretel had ever seen.

The children ran to the cottage and began taking bites from the gingerbread door, pulling off parts of the sweet-covered walls and licking the clear toffee windows.

As they were eating, they heard a soft voice call from inside the house:

'Nibble, nibble, **little** mouse,

Who is nibbling at **my** house?'

Suddenly the door opened and a very old woman came hobbling out. Hansel and Gretel were terribly frightened at first, but the old woman seemed very kind.

'You poor children,' she said, 'You must be starving, come inside and sit by the fire while I make you a **hearty** meal.' She prepared dinner for Hansel and Gretel, and set up two soft beds with thick, warm blankets. The children ate hungrily and then fell fast asleep.

Little did Hansel and Gretel know that although the old woman had been kind to the children, she was actually a *wicked witch* who liked to eat little boys!

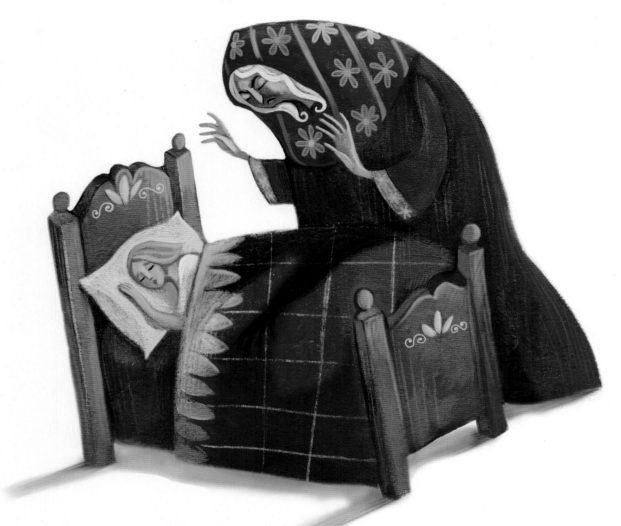

The next morning, while he was still half asleep, the witch seized Hansel and forced him into a cage. **'You will make a pretty mouthful!'** she cackled.

In the following weeks, the witch cooked Hansel all the food he could eat and made Gretel her servant. Because she had terrible eyesight, each morning the witch would make Hansel poke one finger out of the cage so that she could feel how he was fattening up.

But Hansel, being the clever boy he was, had kept a chicken bone from one of his meals and each day he would poke it out of the cage for the witch to feel. She could not understand why he wasn't becoming **plump** and *juicy*!

One day, fed up with waiting for Hansel to fatten up into a *delicious* roast, the witch decided instead to make him into a lovely stew. She made Gretel fetch water and boil it in a big pot with lots of vegetables. The witch sat by cackling cheerfully and rubbing her hands together.

While the stock for the stew was boiling away, the witch ordered Gretel to help her bake some bread.

Gretel kneaded the dough then gave the loaf to the witch, who leaned into the oven to place the bread inside.

Gretel saw her chance – she quickly shoved the witch into the oven and *slammed* the door closed!

'You saved my life!'
Hansel cried, very proud of
his brave sister. Gretel quickly
unlocked Hansel's cage and
set him free.

Quickly, Hansel and Gretel both found large sacks and ran around the house filling them with as much food as they could carry. Gretel also took a large jar of tasty-looking rock candy. They set out into the woods again, *determined* to find their way home.

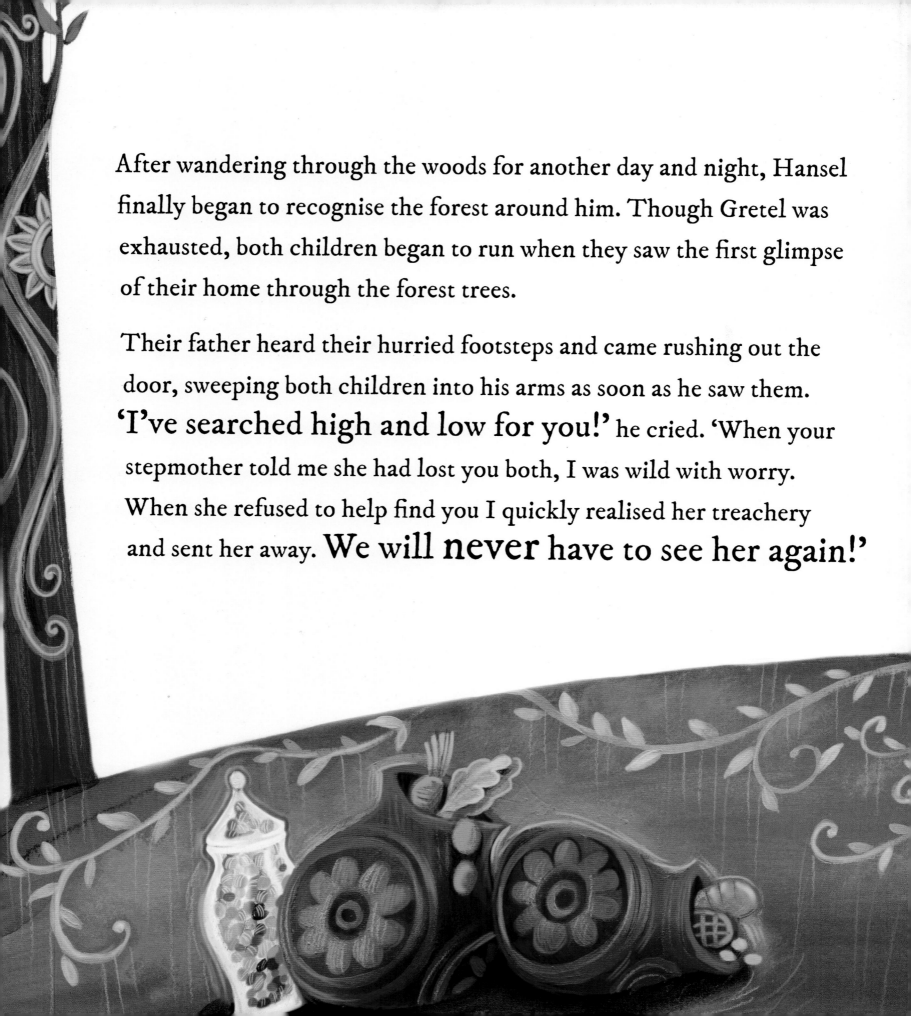

After wandering through the woods for another day and night, Hansel finally began to recognise the forest around him. Though Gretel was exhausted, both children began to run when they saw the first glimpse of their home through the forest trees.

Their father heard their hurried footsteps and came rushing out the door, sweeping both children into his arms as soon as he saw them. **'I've searched high and low for you!'** he cried. 'When your stepmother told me she had lost you both, I was wild with worry. When she refused to help find you I quickly realised her treachery and sent her away. **We will never have to see her again!'**

Inside the house, Hansel and Gretel emptied their sacks and their father was relieved to see there would be enough food to get them through the coming winter. But when Gretel pulled out her jar of rock candy, her father exclaimed. For it turned out that this was not rock candy after all, but precious gems worth a *great fortune*!

So they all lived happily ever after... but Hansel and Gretel never ate sweets again.